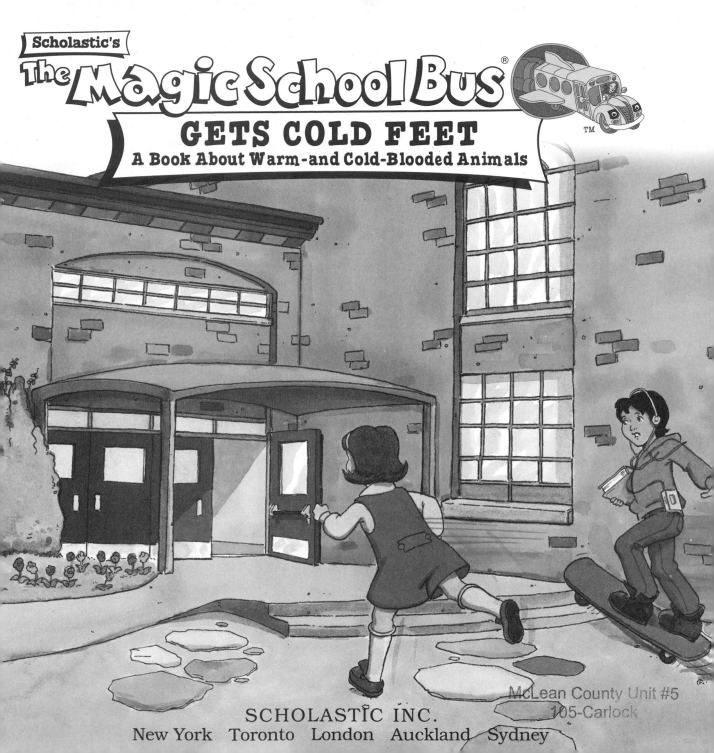

Scholastic's

The Magic School Bus®

GETS COLD FEET
A Book About Warm-and Cold-Blooded Animals

SCHOLASTIC INC.
New York   Toronto   London   Auckland   Sydney

From an episode of the animated TV series
produced by Scholastic Productions, Inc.
Based on *The Magic School Bus* books
written by Joanna Cole and illustrated by Bruce Degen.

TV tie-in adaptation by Tracey West and illustrated by Art Ruiz.
TV script written by Jocelyn Stevenson, John May, and George Bloom.

ISBN 0-590-39724-9

12 11 10   8 9/9 0 1 2/0

Printed in the U.S.A.   24
First Scholastic printing, September 1997

When you're in Ms. Frizzle's class, things never happen the way they're supposed to. Like the other day, when Liz, the class lizard, was missing. We tore up the whole classroom, but we couldn't find her anywhere. Even her habitat was missing!

Maybe she moved into another classroom.

Liz would NEVER leave us!

We were about to give up hope when Ms. Frizzle blew into the room.
She was riding a giant alligator balloon that had sprung a leak.
   "Ms. Frizzle! Liz is missing!" Phoebe cried.
   "Oh, I know," Ms. Frizzle said. "And so is the air from my alligator."
The class was puzzled. Ms. Frizzle didn't seem worried about Liz at all.

Wanda didn't notice. She was busy looking for clues.

"I found a note! It's written in lizard," Wanda cried. "Can you read it, Ms. Frizzle?"

"Let's see," Ms. Frizzle said. "Claw polish, scale moisturizer, fang paste . . ."

"That sounds like a packing list," Tim cried. "Then Liz DID move out!"

Arnold found another clue — a page torn out of a magazine. It showed a picture of a big white building.

"I bet this is where she went," Arnold said. "The address is right here!"

"The place where Liz moved is called Herp Ha," Arnold said.

Wanda shook her head. "The rest of the 'Ha' is torn off," she said. "It's not Herp Ha — it's Herp something else!"

"Okay, but what's a Herp?" Ralphie asked.

Ms. Frizzle smiled. "Good question, Ralphie! Quite simply, a herp is a reptile."

"And Liz is a lizard, which makes her a reptile," Keesha said.

"That still doesn't explain why Liz would pack up and leave us," Wanda said. "She could be in danger. We have to rescue her!"

The bus pulled up to the address. Wanda read the sign in front of the building.

"Herp . . . Haven!" she said. "I told you it wasn't Herp Ha."

"*Haven* means a safe place," said Dorothy Ann.

Ralphie saw another sign. "Yikes! An alligator crossing."

Before the class could get a close look at the alligators, a large car pulled up and a woman got out. She was holding a leash — with a giant tortoise on one end!

Very funny, Mrs. Westlake.

A tall man in a white suit opened the front door.

"I want my tortoise toasted and stuffed, just like the last one," the woman told him.

The class couldn't believe their ears.

"Toasted and stuffed? It sounds like that turtle is about to become somebody's dinner!" Carlos cried.

"What if Liz is next?" Phoebe wailed. "If only we could get inside!"

Wanda tried to get inside, but it didn't work.

The man at the door pulled out a long scroll of paper. "There is a list of requirements that must be met before entry is allowed," he said. "Body temperature: changeable; sweat glands: none; scales or skin: allowed; hair: not allowed. So you see, I cannot let you in. Good day!" He handed Wanda the list and shut the door with a loud bang.

Back on the bus, the class examined the list.

"Body temperature: changeable," Arnold read.

Carlos sighed. "Well, that leaves us out. Our body temperature stays mostly the same."

"That's why we're called WARM-blooded," Keesha said.

Tim looked thoughtful. "Then, is a reptile cold-blooded?"

"All reptiles are cold-blooded!" Ms. Frizzle replied.

Cold-blooded, old-blooded. What we need is a plan!

What we *really* need is a disguise.

Dorothy Ann was reading a book. "I've got it!" she cried. "In ancient times, Greek soldiers built a huge wooden horse and they hid inside it to fool their enemy. It was called a Trojan horse."

"I know!" Phoebe said. "We can turn the bus into a Trojan *alligator*!"

Phoebe stood outside the bus. Ms. Frizzle pulled a lever. *WHOOSH!* Green smoke filled the air. When the smoke cleared, Phoebe saw that the bus had shrunk. It looked just like a life-sized alligator.

"It's a BUS-igator now!" Phoebe cried.

Phoebe put a leash around the busigator and walked up to the front door.

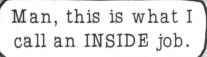

Man, this is what I call an INSIDE job.

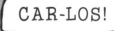

CAR-LOS!

The man in the white suit let Phoebe and the busigator in without a problem.

"What a splendid alligator," the man said. He grabbed the leash. "I'll take her now."

"I should go with her," Phoebe said. "She doesn't like to be alone."

"Don't worry," the man said, leading the busigator away. "We just *love* our cold-blooded critters to death." He left Phoebe all alone.

"Oh, no!" Phoebe moaned. "He's going to toast and stuff the busigator just like that tortoise!"

From inside the busigator, we heard a loud splash.

"We did it!" Wanda cried. "We're in!"

"But where exactly are we?" Ralphie asked.

We looked out of the busigator's front windows. We were in a pool of water near a waterfall. An island filled with shade trees and plants sat just a few feet away. Around the busigator, all kinds of reptiles were crawling — including alligators!

We're in hot water now!

Brrr! Cold water, actually!

"How do we get out of here?" Ralphie asked.

"We can't go out there!" Arnold said nervously. "Those are real snakes and alligators crawling around!"

"We can't find Liz by staying in here," Wanda pointed out.

"If we become reptiles ourselves, we can look for Liz without that guy in white bothering us," Keesha suggested.

Ms. Frizzle smiled. "Good thinking, Keesha!" She walked over to a strange machine built into the bus. It was covered with buttons and flashing lights.

"Kids, meet the Reptilator," the Friz said. "It'll turn us into reptiles in no time."

Um, Ms. Frizzle, maybe I should stay behind and keep an eye on the busigator.

I'll stay with you, Arnold.

Ms. Frizzle pulled a lever. In a flash, we all turned into reptiles — except for Arnold and Dorothy Ann. Carlos was a speckled caiman. Tim was a gecko. Keesha was a garter snake. Wanda was a chameleon. Ralphie was a turtle. And Ms. Frizzle was a frilled lizard.

"I'm cold," Ralphie said, sticking his head inside his shell.

"To get warm, we have to move to a warmer place," Carlos suggested. "Let's try that heat lamp over there."

We all crawled to the lamp.

"It's nice and warm here," Tim said. "I guess to FEEL the heat, you have to FIND the heat."

Meanwhile, Phoebe was trying to find Liz on her own. She checked the kitchen, just in case the man in white was trying to cook Liz for dinner.

Phoebe didn't find Liz, but she did find a weird menu.

"The lizards get just one meal a week?" Phoebe couldn't believe what she was reading. "And the alligators get only one meal a month! How inhumane! What kind of place is this?"

While Phoebe checked out the kitchen, we crawled into the boiler room.

"It really is boiling in here!" Tim said. "So how come I'm not sweating like I usually do when I'm hot?"

"Sweat glands: none!" Wanda said. "That's what it said on the scroll. So I bet reptiles CAN'T sweat to cool down!"

Ralphie stuck his head out of his shell. "If you have to find heat to feel warm, maybe you have to find cold to cool down," he said.

Ms. Frizzle pushed a water bucket toward us. Keesha slithered over to the bucket and stuck her tail in the cold water.

"Wow! I can feel my temperature dropping already!" she exclaimed.

Everyone crawled toward the bucket — except for Wanda.

"We're more worried about staying the right temperature than we are about finding Liz," Wanda said.

Maybe they're upset because we took their heat.

Forget the heat! Let's get back to the bus!

Back at the busigator, Arnold and Dorothy Ann were freezing.

"Let's move the busigator to where it's w-w-warmer," Dorothy Ann chattered.

But the bus wouldn't budge! Arnold and Dorothy Ann left the busigator and tried to push the heat lamp toward it. They didn't go far before Arnold noticed they were being followed — by a swarm of reptiles.

After Ms. Frizzle and we left the boiler room, we crawled into another room. It was cold — very cold. Reptiles were sleeping in glass drawers. A green lizard was curled up in one of them.

"It's Liz!" everyone cried.

"She's barely breathing," Tim noticed.

Keesha put her head near Liz's chest. "I can't hear her heartbeat."

"Wake up, Liz!" Wanda cried.

Ralphie stared at Liz. "She's not sleeping. It looks like she's frozen!"

"There's one thing I don't get," Keesha said. "If it feels so cold, how come I'm not shivering?"

"Reptiles can't shiver," Wanda said. "Shivering is just something people do to get warm."

"Slowing down — isn't that like hibernation?" Keesha asked.

"Exactly," Ms. Frizzle said sleepily.

We were getting sleepier and sleepier when Phoebe walked in.

"When did you guys become reptiles?" she gasped.

Wanda raised her head. "Phoebe! Un . . . hiber . . . nate Liz! Take her some . . . place warm!"

Phoebe grabbed Liz, Ms. Frizzle, and the rest of the class in her arms.

"I'll save you all from this dangerous place!" she said.

. . . ernation . . . isn't . . . ngerous, Phoebe.

Think of it as a . . . va . . . cation.

Phoebe raced out of the cold room. As she warmed up in Phoebe's arms, Liz started to wake up.

Soon, we ran right into the busigator in the reptile habitat!

Wanda looked inside the bus. "Arnold, DA, get us out of here!"

"We c-c-can't," Arnold said. "The bus is so c-c-cold it stopped working."

Ralphie groaned. "If we don't get the bus moving, we could be reptiles for the rest of our lives!"

Liz jumped out of Phoebe's arms and crawled to a nearby heat lamp. A bunch of other reptiles were there, too.

"Look at Liz," Carlos said. "She doesn't look cold anymore. She looks happy!"

"If we get the bus to where it's warmer, it'll start working again," Wanda said.

"I can do that!" Phoebe said. We climbed into the bus, and Phoebe pulled it toward the lamp.

"You can do it, Phoebe!"

With Phoebe's help, we made it to the heat lamp. The busigator warmed up, and pretty soon it was moving again. We followed Phoebe outside. We were free!

Suddenly, a pile of nearby rocks started moving. But they weren't rocks — they were alligators!

"Do something, Ms. Frizzle!" Phoebe yelled.

The Friz pulled some more levers, and soon we all turned back into kids again. The busigator changed back into the size of a regular bus, but now it was a giant lizard! Phoebe climbed aboard.

Just as we were about to escape over the fence, the strange man in white came running after us. He carried something covered by a sheet.

"You forgot something," he said, pulling off the sheet.

"Liz's habitat!" we cried.

Ms. Frizzle shook his hand. "Thanks, Harry."

"You know him?" Phoebe asked.

"Harry Herps is the one who built Liz's habitat," Ms. Frizzle said. "It just needed a few repairs."

"I run Herp Haven," Harry added. "It's a luxury spa and restful resort for weary, worn-out reptiles!"

"So you weren't going to stuff Liz?" Arnold asked.

Harry laughed. "Hardly. But we did make sure she had enough to eat. It wasn't difficult, because reptiles often go for weeks without eating."

"Ms. Frizzle, why didn't you tell us this was a *good* place to be?" Phoebe asked.

The Friz smiled. "I started to tell you, but I just love it when you figure out things for yourselves."

Ms. Frizzle!

Letters from Our Readers

Dear Editor:
What a story! Do you really expect us to believe that there's such a thing as a spa for reptiles? I suppose you're going to say you just made it up so you could show what it's like to be cold-blooded, right? And that handling reptiles like Harry did in the book is dangerous in real life, too, right?

And how come Liz isn't always looking for sunlight and shade to keep herself at the right temperature, like other lizards do? I suppose you're going to say it's because she's a magical lizard, right?

Signed,
Hot Under the Collar

Dear Hot:
You win our award for most cold-blooded letter of the month!
The Editor

Dear Editor:
I just thought you might like to know that reptiles are not the only cold-blooded creatures in the world. Amphibians, fish, and insects are also cold-blooded. In fact, only birds and mammals keep warm from within.
Your pal,
Wyatt Herp

Dear Wyatt:
Your letter warmed my heart!
The Editor

A Note to Parents, Teachers, and Kids

Warm-blooded creatures like me and you don't have to worry about regulating our own temperatures. Our bodies do it for us automatically. But if you were a cold-blooded creature such as a reptile, you'd need to move from place to place to keep yourself at the right temperature. Nothing makes a herp as happy as when the temperature's just right!

Normally, cold-blooded animals do a pretty good job of staying at just the right temperature. But if for some reason it gets too cold around them and they can't move to a warmer place, they might bury themselves under leaves, or find shelter underground — kind of like hibernating.

How else are you different from a cold-blooded animal? Take another look at Harry Herps's list on page 10 to find some ways. Can you think of anything else that makes you different?

Ms. Frizzle